THE SEVEN GO HAUNTING

Enjoy another thrilling adventure with the Secret Seven. They are Peter, Janet, Pam, Colin, George, Jack, Barbara and, of course, Scamper the spaniel.

When Pam and Barbara find a mysterious coded message lying in Mill Lane, the Seven decide to investigate. Their suspicions are confirmed when they receive an anonymous threatening letter; then there is the creepy feeling that they are being watched . . . and the trail of clues leading to a ruined hillside farmhouse. A tense and exciting adventure for all Secret Seven fans.

The Seven Go Haunting

A new adventure of the
characters created by
Enid Blyton, told by Evelyne
Lallemand, translated by
Anthea Bell

Illustrated by Maureen Bradley

KNIGHT BOOKS
Hodder and Stoughton

Copyright © Librairie Hachette
1978

First published in France as
Les Sept sont dans de Beaux Draps

English language translation
copyright © Hodder and
Stoughton Ltd 1984
Illustrations copyright © Hodder
and Stoughton Ltd 1984

First published in Great Britain
by Knight Books 1984
Third impression 1987

British Library C.I.P.

Lallemand, Evelyne
   The Seven go haunting.—
(Knight books)
   I. Title   II. Blyton, Enid
III. Bradley, Maureen   IV. Les
Sept sont dans de beaux draps.
English
843'.914[J]   PZ7

ISBN 0-340-35239-6

Printed and bound in Great
Britain for Hodder and Stoughton
Paperbacks, a division of Hodder
and Stoughton Ltd., Mill Road,
Dunton Green, Sevenoaks, Kent
TN13 2YA. (Editorial Office: 47
Bedford Square, London WC1B
3DP) by Richard Clay Ltd.,
Bungay, Suffolk.

CONTENTS

Chapter One

WHAT CAN THE SECRET SEVEN DO?

'We could put an advertisement in the local paper, I suppose!' said Jack, sighing.

'What — saying "Secret Seven Society Seeks Mystery or Adventure", you mean?' asked Peter, laughing. 'And telling people to send any interesting suggestions to The Garden Shed, Old Mill House!'

'Oh, very funny!' said Jack sarcastically. 'Very funny indeed! But what are we going to *do*?'

'Well, I expect we'll have to stop being a Society if nothing interesting happens to us!'

The two boys were at a loose end. They were sitting in the sun on a little wall at the end of Peter and Janet's garden. Peter's father had a farm, and the farmhouse was called Old Mill House, after the ruined mill which stood on a hill some way off. It was a fine morning in late September. There were clumps of bright dahlias and asters in the flower-beds, and the first windfall apples had a delicious, autumny sort of smell.

Scamper, the golden spaniel, was lying at the boys' feet. He stretched, lazily.

'You need exercise,' Peter told the dog.

As if he understood, Scamper stood up on his hind legs and laid his head on his young master's knees.

'Scamper, old boy, it looks as if the Secret Seven Society's coming to an end!' Peter told him.

'That's what my sister Susie keeps on saying,' Jack said gloomily. 'She says we're done for – and *I* keep telling her we're not. No, Peter, we're jolly well not!'

'All right, all right, Jack — calm down!' Peter told his friend. 'Look, here come the girls. *They* seem to have found something to do.'

Pam and Barbara had just come round the corner of the road. They saw the two boys and came towards them. They were pushing a wheelbarrow full of litter.

'Hallo!' called Pam. 'Any news? I mean, has anything interesting happened?'

'Not yet,' said Peter and Jack sadly.

'Then why not come and help us?' Barbara suggested. 'That won't leave you any time to be bored.'

The two girls had reached the garden gate. Scamper recognised them and ran up the path to give them a warm welcome.

'Phew!' sighed Pam, putting down the wheelbarrow. 'I need a rest! You've no idea what a lot of litter there is to be picked up. People really are awful. Just look at all this rubbish — and we've only been down three roads so far!'

'There ought to be litter-bins in the village,' said Peter.

'My father told me it *was* suggested at the parish council meeting,' Barbara said. 'But the councillors voted against the idea — they thought it would cost more than it was worth.'

'I suppose the councillors would rather go slipping on banana skins!' said Pam crossly.

Peter agreed with her. He felt sure that if *he* were on the parish council, he'd soon make them see sense!

'They could have litter-bins painted in nice bright colours, so they'd look good as well as being useful,' said Jack.

'Well, all I know is that they decided not to,' said Barbara. 'So now it's up to us to keep the village tidy.'

And she picked up both handles of the wheel-barrow and started off again.

'By the way, where's Janet?' Pam asked the boys, before she followed her friend. 'She said she'd come out with Barbara and me this morning and help us.'

'Mother made her stay at home to help with the housework,' said Peter. 'But I expect she'll join you this afternoon.'

'Fine!' said Pam, and she ran off after Barbara.

Peter and Jack watched the girls walk away. They went on sitting on the wall in silence for a few minutes. The sunlight and silence in the garden made them feel quite sleepy. Scamper had come back to lie at their feet again – and he actually *was* asleep.

Then they heard a voice. It was Peter's mother calling.

'Peter! Peter – are you there? Have you got any change?'

Peter jumped off the wall and ran up the garden path, followed by Jack. His mother was standing in the doorway.

'Someone's come collecting for the blind, and I've only got a five-pound note,' Mother explained. 'Can you lend me any change?'

'Oh – I'll go and look in the Secret Seven Society's treasury and see what we've got,' said Peter.

He went into the shed and over to a shelf holding several upturned flowerpots. Jack waited in the shed doorway, watching him search the shelf and grinning.

'Now, which flowerpot *did* we put it under?' muttered Peter. 'It's so long since we had a meeting – whose bright idea was it to hide the purse under a flowerpot, anyway?'

'George's. After all, he *is* our treasurer,' Jack reminded him. 'Perhaps he was hoping the money in the purse would grow, like seeds!'

'Oh, good, here it is,' said Peter.

He had to blow a lot of dust off the leather purse. It tickled his nose. Then he and Jack went back up the garden to his mother, and all three of them went into the house.

A young man was standing in the hall, holding a collecting-box.

'Here you are,' said Peter's mother. 'Luckily my son can lend me some change.'

'Oh, that's very kind of you,' said the collector, smiling at Peter.

Peter's mother had borrowed a fifty-pence piece, and she put it into the collecting-box.

'Thank you very much, madam,' said the young man, jingling the money in his box. 'It all goes to the blind, so it really is a very good cause.'

11

Then he said goodbye and left the house.

'We had someone collecting at *our* house yesterday, too,' said Jack. 'He was rather nice – but I didn't much like the look of *this* one just now.'

'That just goes to show you shouldn't judge by appearances,' said Peter's mother, going into the kitchen.

'Yes – you must admit it's awfully good of people to spend the whole day going round knocking at doors,' said Peter. 'I'm sure they don't always get such a friendly response as here.'

Suddenly the doorbell rang hard. Ding, ding, ding!

Peter hurried to open the door. There stood Pam and Barbara. The two girls were quite out of breath.

'Quick!' cried Barbara. 'We must have a special meeting of the Society!'

'What's up?' exclaimed the boys.

'We'll tell you in the shed. Not here!' Pam said firmly.

'All right,' Peter decided. 'Let's go straight to the shed, then.'

'Who's that?' someone called from upstairs.

'Pam and Barbara,' said Peter. 'We're going out to the shed!'

They immediately heard footsteps running downstairs, and Janet appeared, holding a duster in her hand. She hugged the girls. 'Oh!' she said. 'I wish I could come too, but I'm afraid I haven't finished the housework yet!'

But luckily the kitchen door was ajar, and Mother had overheard the whole conversation. 'That's all right, dear—you run along with the others,' she said.

And off they went. Once the door of the shed was firmly bolted, Pam could speak freely.

'Look what we found in Mill Lane just now!'

And she showed Peter a piece of lined paper torn out of a notebook. Jack and Janet looked over his shoulder so that they could read it too. A few words and figures were scribbled on the paper, in black ink: '2829 g.sh. 1.till'.

'What on earth does that nonsense mean?' said Jack, baffled.

'Something sinister, I'm sure!' said Barbara. 'I

don't think it's nonsense – I think it's only meant to *look* like nonsense.'

'Why?' asked Peter.

'Well – if the person who wrote this message didn't have something to hide, wouldn't he have put it more clearly?'

'You see, it's probably in code,' Pam added. ' "2829 g." – well, maybe in gangster language that says some-one's going to drop a bomb on the village, or rob the bank, or . . .'

'Or what?' said Peter, laughing. 'I say – you two *have* got a lot of imagination, haven't you?'

'Oh, honestly, you're hopeless!' said Pam crossly. 'When we might be able to stop a crime being com-mitted – and all you can say is that we've got too much imagination!'

'Pam's right!' said Janet, speaking up for her friend. 'We may not be able to understand this note, but we can't just ignore it. The Society hasn't had anything to do for weeks – so this is our chance to go into action!'

'Yes – we can at least try to puzzle out what the note *does* mean,' suggested Jack. 'Then we can decide if it's anything serious, and if it's worth doing some-thing about it.'

'All right,' said Peter. 'I agree. We don't want to let our brains wither right away, just because nothing much is happening. So let's try to solve the puzzle of this message. Who knows, it might lead to an adventure!'

'Hurrah for adventures!' cried Jack and the three girls.

The Seven really loved adventures! Once again, the children thought, they'd show how good they were at solving problems – and their first problem was this mysterious message.

Chapter Two

THE MYSTERIOUS MESSAGE

They set to work on it at once – just the five of them, because they had decided not to tell George and Colin, the other two members of the Secret Seven Society, until they'd deciphered the code. They didn't want to raise any false hopes.

First, they went over the writing on the paper again and again, looking at it in every way they could think of. But alas, the words and figures just didn't seem to make sense. Then the children decided to try replacing the figures by the corresponding letters of the alphabet. That gave them 'B H B I' – which still didn't make sense. But as their hopes were fading, Peter had a bright idea. It set them off on another track.

'*I* think we're trying to be too clever,' he said. 'Look at that note again – it's not a very educated person's handwriting, is it? I'm sure the writer of the message would never have thought up all the complicated ideas we're imagining.'

'Peter's right,' agreed Pam. 'Now, let's see – what does 2829 make you think of?'

'Not the Battle of Hastings, anyway!' said Jack, laughing.

'Oh dear — it could be almost anything!' sighed Janet. 'Two thousand eight hundred and twenty-nine metres, two thousand eight hundred and twenty-nine seconds —'

'Oh, Janet, you've just given me an idea!' cried Barbara. 'Listen — it could be an appointment for a meeting. A meeting due to take place at the two thousand eight hundred and twenty-ninth second of the day! If we divide by sixty . . .'

Quickly, she scribbled a sum down on a scrap of paper.

'Well, that would be forty-seven minutes and nine seconds after midnight,' she said.

'No, that's still too complicated,' said Peter. 'Let's try something simpler. I like your idea of a meeting, though, Barbara. Let's go on thinking along those lines.'

'If only there were more than twenty-four hours in the day!' said Jack. 'Then it could mean 28 hours 29 minutes.'

'Oh, brilliant!' said Pam sarcastically. 'Look — suppose it isn't two thousand eight hundred and twenty-nine anything? Suppose it's a twenty-eight followed by a twenty-nine?'

'I know!' cried Janet. 'It's a date. What's the date today?'

Peter looked at his watch. It was a new one, and he

was very proud of it, because it was the kind which shows you the date as well as the time of day.

'It's the twenty-eighth!' he said in surprise. 'Oh, I see! The numbers could mean the meeting's been fixed for in between today and tomorrow . . .'

'Yes – on the stroke of midnight!' finished Barbara.

'I *told* you the note looked like the start of an adventure!' cried Pam excitedly.

But the children's pleasure in their discovery didn't last long. When they tried working out what the letters meant, they still couldn't get any further.

'G.sh.l.till,' Barbara kept on saying.

'It must mean somewhere near here,' said Jack.

'G as in gram!' said Pam. 'Sh as in – oh, as in shut up. L for lion. Shut up lion? Lion is shut up?'

'Wait a minute!' said Janet. 'I've had another idea. L could be short for pounds. And sh could be short for shillings — what people had before there were new pence. Grandma keeps saying that she still thinks of money as "l.s.d.", and people like her are too old to change their ways. Well, suppose this note is saying there's going to be a robbery in the village.'

'No,' said Peter, after thinking this idea over. 'That's no good, I'm afraid, Janet — it's still too complicated. I mean, pounds, shillings and pence went out ages ago. We'd have to assume the burglars were all Grandma's age! And anyway the sh and the l would be the wrong way round. And then there's the g at one end of the message and the till at the other.

18

Till *when*?'

'Yes, what *can* it mean?' said Barbara. 'Whatever the message is, it seems to have stopped dead in the middle of what it was saying!'

They were interrupted by the sound of steps coming down the garden path towards the shed.

'Janet, dear!' Mother called through the wooden door. 'It's nearly lunchtime – would you go down to the grocer's shop for me?'

'*Shop*!' gasped Jack. 'Shop!' he shouted at the top of his voice. 'That sh is short for shop! G.sh. – grocer's shop!'

'Whatever are you children playing at now?' asked Mother. 'Fancy shutting yourselves up in that shed to play word games on such a fine, sunny day! Now, if we're going to have any lunch, Janet, I want you to go down to Mr Dunning's and buy a bottle of salad cream while I wash the lettuce.'

Rather reluctantly, Janet left the shed and ran off to the grocer's.

Peter closed the door after her – and he and the other three went on talking more excitedly than ever.

'Jack's right!' said Barbara. 'Someone's planning a burglary at the grocer's shop!'

'G.sh. – grocer's shop,' Pam repeated. 'L – well, never mind that now. Oh, wait – *till*! Now it makes sense. It doesn't mean *till* a certain time. It's a shop-keeper's till!'

'Yes, now we're getting somewhere!' said Peter.

'But what can the l. mean?' Barbara wondered out loud.

'I know – it could be something to do with the *lock* of the till!' Jack announced.

'That's it!' said Peter. 'Mr Dunning *has* got a locking till in his shop. The burglars are after his takings – and they're planning to break into the shop this very night. There's not a moment to lose! Let's tell George and Colin, and then go to the grocer's and warn him!'

Chapter Three

MORE CLUES

Peter and Janet simply gobbled down their lunch. As soon as they had finished the last mouthful of their cold ham and salad, they asked their mother if they could take an apple each instead of pudding and go straight out, and off they ran, followed by the faithful Scamper.

Peter had decided that the Seven would all meet at the spot where Pam and Barbara had found the mysterious message, before they went to warn Mr Dunning. He thought it would be a good idea to have a look at the 'scene of the crime', so that when he talked to the grocer and warned him he was going to be burgled, it would sound more convincing.

With Scamper at their heels, Peter and Janet reached Mill Lane in a couple of minutes – as you can guess from the name, it wasn't far from their home, Old Mill House. It was a narrow alley with high walls on either side.

Jack and Barbara, George and Colin were there waiting. Pam was the last to arrive, as usual!

'I've told George and Colin all about it,' said Jack, 'so we can begin our investigations at once!'

'Hold on!' said Colin. 'One thing you haven't told us is what makes you so sure it's Mr Dunning who's going to be burgled? There are two other shops selling groceries in the village, after all. There's Mrs White's general stores — and the post office sells eggs and tinned food and several other things like that.'

Peter had to admit that they'd never actually stopped to ask themselves that question, because when Mother asked Janet to go down to Mr Dunning's, the answer seemed so obvious. Luckily, Barbara could think of another good reason!

'Well, Mr Dunning is the only one whose shop has a till that can be locked,' she explained. 'Don't you remember how proud he was when he first got that locking till? Though I don't suppose the lock will worry the burglars — they're probably planning to break it open.'

That satisfied Colin. The Seven walked on down Mill Lane.

'It was just here we found the piece of paper with the message,' said Barbara, pointing to the side of the road. 'Down in the grass there.'

They all bent down to look at the spot. Even Scamper set to work, sniffing busily.

'Look!' said Peter. 'The grass is all crushed. Whoever wrote the message was here for some time.'

'Whoever was *carrying* the message, you mean,'

George corrected him. 'We don't know if it was the same person who *wrote* it.'

'I've found some cigarette ends,' said Janet, who had gone a little farther on. 'Lots of them, in fact – there are cigarette ends everywhere!'

The others hurried to join her. Peter picked up one of the cigarette ends. There were about a dozen of them, all the same, with a gold ring near the end. There was a torn-off bit of cigarette packet lying in the grass too.

'It's a brand called Wessex Cigarettes,' said Peter.

Jack started slightly, although he didn't mean to.

'I thought you two girls had picked up all the litter lying around,' Colin said, teasing Pam and Barbara.

Pam flared up angrily. 'Well, we stopped when we found the note, of course! Any objections?' she asked sharply.

'Now then, that'll do, you two!' Peter told them. Pam and Colin were always quarrelling with each other. It could be annoying for the rest of the Seven – but thanks to their little tiff, Jack had managed to hide his alarm from his friends. He knew it was silly, but he couldn't help feeling he had a guilty secret when Peter said what the brand of cigarettes was – because his father smoked Wessex Cigarettes too!

'Mind where you tread!' called Barbara. 'I've found some footprints on the ground beside this wall.'

'Very clear ones, too,' said Peter, pleased. 'The

rain we had yesterday made the ground quite soft. It's taken the shape of the footprints just like Plasticine!'

'Why don't we make moulds of the prints?' suggested George.

'Yes – plaster casts,' said Janet. 'I'm sure they'd make super plaster casts. I've never *seen* such clear footprints before.'

'All right,' said Peter. 'What do *you* think, Jack? You're rather quiet this afternoon.'

'Oh, I think it's a fine idea,' Jack said quickly. 'And we've got some plaster in the shed, so we don't need to buy any!'

Peter decided on their immediate plan of action.

'George and Colin, you're both good with your hands. You take the plaster casts.'

The two boys nodded.

'And you girls,' went on the head of the Secret Seven, 'can go to the tobacconist's, and any other shops selling cigarettes, and see if you can find out who lives in the village and smokes Wessex Cigarettes.'

Jack almost said, 'My father does!' But he didn't quite dare. He hated to think of his father being mixed up in all this – and his name would be sure to come up when they were making a list of suspects, because he smoked quite a lot, and he usually bought his cigarettes at the village shops. All sorts of horrible thoughts were going round and round in poor Jack's

24

head.

'And Jack and I will go and warn Mr Dunning,' Peter finished.

'Woof! Wuff, wuff – woof!'

'All right, Scamper – you can come too!' said Peter, laughing.

But that wasn't what Scamper had meant!

He was running towards the end of the lane – and the Seven saw Jack's sister Susie and her friend Binkie standing there. They had been spying!

'Oh, those awful pests!' said Janet crossly.

'My word – they must have radar or something!' said Colin. 'We started our investigation less than an hour ago, and they're on our trail already.'

For once, Jack didn't join in the angry outcry. He usually thought Susie was dreadfully tiresome, but now he had other worries. His lively imagination kept showing him pictures of his father burgling the grocer's shop, getting arrested by the police, and finally being put in prison!

Scamper reached the end of the lane and chased the two little girls away. He came back to the Seven looking very proud of himself.

'Right!' said Peter. 'Off we go! We'll meet in the shed at six o'clock this evening and make our reports. The new password is "Wessex"!'

The children divided into their three groups and set off in different directions. What would they discover?

Chapter Four

MR DUNNING

Mr Dunning's shop was certainly the main grocery shop in the village. It was in the High Street, and had two big plate-glass windows. When Peter and Jack got there, they looked in through one of the windows and could see that Mr Dunning was serving an old lady they knew, Mrs Lea.

'We'd better wait till he's on his own,' Peter decided. 'After all, there's no need for the whole village to know what's up – the burglars might be warned off, too!'

The two boys had to be very patient, because Mrs Lea couldn't seem to make up her mind which sort of tinned peas she wanted. At last she decided, and bought a tin. They watched her pay, saw Mr Dunning put the money into his till – *the* till! – and then she went to the door. What a relief when they heard the jangle of the doorbell! But Mrs Lea still had to go down three steps before she had really left the shop – and it took her at least ten minutes to get down those steps. All this time Mr Dunning was standing in the doorway of his shop, listening politely as his customer chattered away.

Peter and Jack were standing only a short way off, simply seething with impatience. 'A nice fine day today,' Mrs Lea was saying, 'but there's a bit of a nip in the air in the mornings. Did you hear about the flood they had at Covelty after that storm the other day?'

Peter and Jack thought she would go on about the weather all afternoon! But then they had a stroke of luck. Miss Adair, an old friend of Mrs Lea's, came walking down the road. The two old ladies said hallo to each other, and decided to go home together.

'At last!' whispered Jack. 'The coast's clear!'

A couple of seconds later, he and Peter were going through the door of the grocer's shop. Mr Dunning might have a fine modern till, but he had the nice sort of old-fashioned bell that jingles as you walk through a shop doorway. He smiled at the boys when he saw them come in.

'And what can I do for you two?' he asked, going to stand behind his counter.

'Er — we want a word with you,' Peter began, feeling a little awkward. He was afraid the grocer wouldn't take him seriously.

'It's like this,' said Jack. 'We've come to give you a warning!'

'A warning? Goodness me! A warning of what, may I ask?' said the grocer. He sounded surprised, but he was still smiling.

Looking very grave, Peter got the piece of paper with the mysterious message on it out of his pocket. He showed it to Mr Dunning.

'Read that!' he said.

The grocer read the note. 'What on earth is this nonsense?' he asked.

'It's not nonsense,' said Peter. 'There's a plot to burgle your shop!'

'Yes — and the burglars are planning to break in this very night!' added Jack.

'Oh, are they really?' Mr Dunning sounded sarcastic, and to their dismay, Peter and Jack saw that he was cross with them. 'I'm sure you're good lads at heart,' the grocer added, 'but don't you come telling *me* any of your tall tales! Now, get out of my shop and go and play your silly games somewhere else!'

Peter took several deep breaths so as to stay relaxed. If the grocer was losing his temper, that made things more difficult, and *he* must be sure not to lose *his*!

'You see, 2829 means twenty-eight, twenty-nine, and the rest of the message means "grocery shop, locking till",' he explained.

'Twenty-eight and twenty-nine mean that something is going to happen in between today and tomorrow,' Jack added. 'Which means midnight tonight!'

'And when people are coming to somewhere

there's a till at midnight,' said Peter, 'it's not usually just to stand and admire its beauty!'

'What on earth *are* you talking about?' asked Mr Dunning. 'Are you telling me someone's got designs on the money in my till?'

'Yes — that's *exactly* what we're telling you,' said Peter.

The grocer read the puzzling message for the second time — and a change came over the expression on his face.

'Mine certainly *is* the only grocer's shop in this village with a locking till,' he said rather proudly. 'There may be some truth in this tale of yours!'

'It's *all* true!' said Peter earnestly.

'What are you going to *do* about it?' asked Jack, who felt time was running short.

But before Mr Dunning could reply, the shop doorbell jingled again, and in came old Mr Long, bent double under the weight of his shopping basket. He was smoking a pipe, and soon the shop was full of the old man's tobacco smoke. It had a nice smell, rather like honey.

'I'll be with you in just a minute, Mr Long,' said Mr Dunning politely. 'I'll show these young men out, and then I'll be back!'

'Oh, that's quite all right, Mr Dunning,' said Mr Long. 'No hurry! I've got all the time in the world, now I'm retired.'

He seemed quite happy to stand there, looking at

the carefully arranged display of chocolate bars on the counter, so Mr Dunning went to the shop door with Peter and Jack. He must have been making up his mind quickly – when they were out on the steps down to the pavement, he told them in a low voice, 'I'll telephone the police station at once. And if anyone's thinking of coming to take a look at my till tonight, well, they'll be in for quite a surprise! Because I'll be waiting up for them!'

'Good!' said Peter, shaking the grocer's hand. 'We'll come round tomorrow to hear what happens.'

'Yes, do that, boys! I'll see you tomorrow, then – and thanks!'

And Mr Dunning went back into the shop to serve old Mr Long, who was still standing there dreamily smoking his pipe.

Peter and Jack felt pleased – they'd done what they set out to do. It wasn't six o'clock yet, so they decided to go back to Mill Lane before meeting the other children back at the shed.

They found Scamper on guard at the end of the lane, acting like a fierce watchdog! The good spaniel was standing there barking at anyone but the Secret Seven who wanted to go down the lane. Susie and Binkie had been snooping yet again, trying to find out just what George and Colin were doing, and Scamper had been posted there to keep them away.

He was still at his post when Peter and Jack reached Mill Lane.

'That's a good boy!' said Peter, going over to pat the spaniel.

Scamper was feeling very friendly, and had to have a bit of a fuss made of him before he would let even

Peter into the lane! Then he gave two loud barks, to let George and Colin know they had visitors.

Peter and Jack went down the lane to join their friends. They found Colin sprinkling talcum powder over one of the footprints that showed so clearly on the soft ground. George was standing beside him, ready to cover the footprint with a shovelful of freshly mixed plaster.

'This is the last footprint,' he told Jack and Peter. 'We've taken casts of about a dozen of them.' And he emptied his shovel over the neatly powdered footprint.

'The others are drying off in the shed,' said Colin. 'They're very good casts too – just wait and see!'

'What's the talcum powder for?' asked Jack.

'Oh – that's to dry off the ground,' said Colin. 'And it makes it easier to lift the cast away.'

'You two really are experts!' said Peter admiringly. 'Has anyone come along and disturbed you?'

'No, not since we put Scamper on guard,' said George. 'He's an awfully good watchdog!'

Colin scratched the plaster with his fingernail, to see if it had set.

'We can take the cast off in a minute or so,' he said.

'How did you two get on?' asked George. 'What did Mr Dunning say?'

'George, you know perfectly well we're going to discuss all that at our meeting in the shed!' said Peter sternly. 'I can't stand saying the same thing over and over again. And we might be overheard if I told you out in the open here.'

Poor George! He didn't see why Peter had to speak to him so sharply.

'Peter's right!' Colin joked, with mock solemnity. 'I bet there are at least ten spies lurking behind these walls, with microphones to pick up everything we say.'

Jack and George both laughed, but Peter was cross. He didn't like it when anyone seemed to be challenging his authority as head of the Secret Seven. He looked at his watch and said in a chilly sort of voice that it was five to six, and then he strode away from Mill Lane without waiting for the others.

'I say – Peter's in a bad temper this evening!' said Colin. 'Can't he take a joke? Honestly, if he's going on like this I'll . . .' Then he stopped suddenly.

'You'll what?' asked Jack.

Colin *had* been going to say that he'd leave the Secret Seven Society – but he knew he didn't really want to, so what was the point of saying so? It would only be an empty threat. He certainly didn't like the idea of anyone else taking his place! Suppose the others let Susie join? She was always pestering them to be allowed into the Society – and however hard Jack explained to his sister that a Secret Seven Society *couldn't* have more than seven members, she wouldn't take no for an answer.

'Oh, nothing!' said Colin. 'I was only thinking that

34

life's not much fun without a sense of humour!'

'Hear, hear!' said George, and they all followed Peter off to the shed. It was going to be an interesting meeting!

Chapter Five

A MEETING OF THE SECRET SEVEN

The church clock struck six.

'Wessex!' said Jack, in a low voice.

The door of the shed opened, and Jack, Colin and George went in. The girls were there already. Jack couldn't help thinking that by now they must have discovered that his father always smoked Wessex Cigarettes.

As soon as Peter had bolted the door, he began to speak. 'Now, we'll all make our reports! First, Mr Dunning. Well, Jack and I went to warn him, and we managed to make him take us seriously. He said he'd tell the police and stay on watch in his shop tonight. We're going to call on him tomorrow and find out what happened. Next, those footprints in Mill Lane. George — would *you* like to tell us about that?'

He gave George a friendly grin. The fact was, Peter was just a little ashamed of himself for losing his temper with his friend, and this was his way of apologising. George was a good sport! He smiled back at Peter, and began his own report.

'We've taken thirteen casts of the footprints.

Here's the last one – it isn't quite dry yet. The others are up on that shelf behind you, and in a moment you can all have a look at them. But first I want to tell you what we've discovered!'

George paused dramatically. What he had to say must be very important! His friends all leaned towards him, listening intently. Even Scamper pricked up his ears!

'There are *two* sorts of footprints, not just one!' he announced. 'That means there will probably be at least two people trying to break into Mr Dunning's till tonight — so it's just as well he's warned the police.'

'Golly!' said Peter. This was getting really exciting! 'Let's see the prints!'

'Would you pass the casts over, Barbara?' asked Colin. 'They're just behind you.'

Barbara turned round, picked up the twelve plaster casts one by one, and handed them out to the rest of the Seven. The casts were about the size of bricks, and each of them showed a very distinct footprint on one side.

'I say — did you notice the big ridges on the sole of this shoe?' asked Pam. 'I should think it's really a boot rather than a shoe!'

'Yes, it's the kind of sole you get on hill-walking boots,' Jack agreed.

'This print's different,' said Colin, holding up the cast he had taken last of all, so that everyone could see it. 'We only found three prints like it.'

'Oh — I've got the second here!' said Peter.

'Yes, and here's the third,' added Janet. 'The sole is smoother than that other one with all the ridges.'

'I think the print was made by a Wellington boot,' said Colin. 'See that little shield shape on it? I'm sure I've seen it on the soles of Wellingtons.'

Peter held up his cast to get a good look at it. 'There's something written on the sole, too — it must be the brand name, but I can't make out what it says.'

'I can!' cried Janet. 'Look – it's come out quite clearly on *my* cast! F – I – yes, that's it! FISHERMAN!'

Fisherman! Jack's heart began to thump. His father wore Fisherman boots. Poor Jack! He felt as if he were caught in a trap. He could just imagine all the things people at school would say – the questions they'd ask about his father, the sarcastic comments they'd make! And yet he was sure, at heart, that his father had nothing to do with the plan to burgle Mr Dunning's shop.

Then Pam said, quite simply. 'Oh, my father has a pair of Fisherman brand Wellington boots!'

'Yes, it's quite a popular make,' Colin agreed. 'Not much chance of tracking down the criminals that way!'

'We can't actually talk about criminals yet,' Peter pointed out, 'since the crime hasn't been committed. We'll have to wait until midnight! Now, let's have the third report. What did you girls find out?'

'Not an awful lot,' said Janet. 'There aren't many people in the village who smoke Wessex Cigarettes – the tobacconist told us they were rather a special taste, and he only has three regular customers for that brand.'

'One of them is my father!' Jack managed to say, in a rather shaky voice.

'That's right,' Janet agreed. So the girls *had* found

39

out, just as Jack expected! 'The three regular customers are your father, and the police inspector and Mr Dunning himself!'

Well, that didn't make Jack feel any better! Barbara noticed that he seemed worried.

'There's no need to be upset, Jack,' she said. 'Obviously no one would suspect your father – any more than they'd suspect the inspector or Mr Dunning!'

'Of course not!' George agreed.

'Don't be such a donkey, Jack!' Peter said, teasing his friend. 'What *were* you thinking of?'

At that Jack smiled! It was really cheering to find that his friends were so loyal. All the worries that had been tormenting him through the afternoon suddenly seemed stupid.

He said boldly, 'Well, my father has a pair of Fisherman boots as well! So you can see that our suspects, whoever they are, are just like any ordinary person – what's called the man in the street! That doesn't make things any easier for us.'

'Mr Dunning should have something to tell us tomorrow morning, though,' Peter reminded him. 'We only have to wait till then!'

The Seven had trouble dropping off to sleep that evening. All of them were wondering what was going on in the grocer's shop, as Mr Dunning waited up for his unwanted visitors.

Next day Peter and Jack met, as they had arranged to do, to go to the grocer's shop before school. But when they got there, they were surprised to see the metal shutters still down over the big plate-glass windows.

'I wonder what happened?' said Jack. 'I know the shop's usually open at this time of the morning – I always pass it on my way to school! Mr Dunning opens early so that people can drop in and buy bottled drinks and so on to keep for their lunch.'

'Something awful must have happened last night!' said Peter.

They were feeling quite frightened, hoping poor Mr Dunning was all right. The two boys began hammering on the metal shutters with their fists.

That made a terrible noise – and in a moment or so an upstairs window opened.

'Oh, it's you kids, is it?' said an unfriendly voice.

There was Mr Dunning, standing at the window in a pair of striped pyjamas.

'You do me out of a good night's rest with your silly stories – and to add insult to injury, you come to wake me up first thing in the morning! You can just clear off, or I'll come down and give you what for!'

Peter and Jack were astonished! The grocer was certainly in a terrible temper with them – but why?

'We haven't done anything to you!' Peter protested indignantly. 'In fact, just the opposite! We came and warned you!'

'Warned me, eh? Didn't warn me it was all one of your silly hoaxes, did you? I sat up all night, and so did the inspector – if *he* catches you, you'd better watch out! He'd like to give you kids a good hiding!'

'But . . . but we found that message!' said Jack.

'Found it? Made it up, more like!'

Jack opened his mouth to deny the accusation, but Mr Dunning wasn't in any mood to listen. He had picked up a pot of geraniums standing on his window sill and was threatening the boys with it. His face was as red as the geraniums themselves!

'Mind what you say!' shouted the angry grocer.

'Come on!' Peter whispered to his friend. 'It's no use talking to him!'

42

The two boys went off—and Mr Dunning slammed his window shut and went back to bed!

Chapter Six

THE ANONYMOUS LETTER

Outside the gates of the boys' school, a young man was jingling a collecting-box. If you stopped to read what the box said, you could see he was collecting for deprived children.

Quite a lot of the parents who were bringing their sons to school did stop to see what the collection was for, and put something in the box. A few of the schoolchildren themselves had some odd change in their pockets. They too put it into the box the collector was holding out.

By the time Peter and Jack arrived at the gates, however, the bell had rung and there was no one out on the pavement except the young collector. He was just moving off as the two boys arrived. They noticed him as they passed.

'That's the man who came collecting at our house the other day,' said Jack.

Then they realised they'd have to hurry if they were to get to their classroom on time – so they put on a sprint, just managed to slip into their places with-

out anyone noticing they were a minute late, and forgot about the man with the collecting-box.

Nothing out of the ordinary happened at school that day. However, the Seven had lots to discuss! They could hardly wait to meet in the garden shed that evening.

'I tell you what – the burglars didn't carry out their plan because they realised we knew about it!' said Colin.

45

'They *can't* have done!' Pam objected. 'I mean, it's impossible! We were being so careful not to give anything away. You can't blame me and the other girls — we made sure we went into the back of the tobacconist's and the other shops we visited before we asked any questions. And you and George said you didn't see anyone in Mill Lane, Colin!'

'That's right,' George agreed. 'We didn't see a soul. And Scamper was on guard at the end of the lane to let us know when anyone was coming.'

'Are you sure no one could have overheard you talking to the grocer?' Colin asked Peter and Jack.

'Quite sure — we waited till Mrs Lea had left,' said Jack.

'Wait a minute!' said Peter. 'Old Mr Long did come in while we were talking to Mr Dunning. *He* might have overheard the end of what we were telling him. But it's hard to think of him in league with a gang of burglars.'

'Anyway, he smokes a pipe,' Jack reminded his friend. 'So that means he can't be one of our cigarette-smoking burglars!'

And that seemed to be that. The Seven were face to face with a real mystery. There was silence in the garden shed for several minutes. The children were all feeling very gloomy.

Then, suddenly, Scamper made a frantic dash for the door! To their surprise, the Seven saw a white envelope being pushed underneath it. A perfectly ordinary envelope – but what could it contain?

Peter pounced on it like lightning, while Colin and Jack dashed out of the shed.

It was pitch dark in the garden. Night fell early now that autumn had come.

'Look – over there!' shouted Colin. 'I can see some-body running away!'

Sure enough, a shadowy figure was just dis-appearing through the hedge. The branches of some of the bushes were still quivering!

Colin ran across the garden, with Scamper at his heels.

'Quick – he got out into the road!' he shouted to Jack, who was following.

Five seconds later, the two boys were out in the road themselves – but it was deserted.

'Oh, blow! He got away!' said Colin, panting for breath.

But Scamper was still growling softly – and suddenly the spaniel shot off again. There was a street light on the corner of the road. A moment later Susie and Binkie appeared under the light. Colin and Jack ran over to them.

'Hallo, what's all the hurry?' asked that little nuisance Binkie.

'Did you see anybody a moment ago?' Jack asked his sister.

'Yes, a man running very fast,' said Susie. 'Is that who you mean?'

'Yes, it is! Where was he going? Which way did he turn at the crossroads? What did he look like?'

'My goodness – that's a lot of questions all at once!' said Susie, laughing.

Jack had to make a great effort not to lose his temper with her. 'Come on, *tell* us!' he said.

'You'll never catch up with him! He was going awfully fast!'

'Which *way* was he going?' Colin asked again.

At last Binkie gave the boys an answer. 'He turned into Mill Lane,' she said.

'What did he look like?' Jack repeated. 'Come on, do try to remember!'

Binkie just shrugged her shoulders, but Susie said, 'He was wearing jeans, and a leather jacket.'

'What was his face like?' cried Jack excitedly. 'Have you ever seen him before?'

'No, never,' said Susie. 'I'd have thought he was quite young – but I may be wrong, because it was awfully dark where he passed us.'

'Is that all you can tell us?' asked Jack.

'Yes, that's all,' said Susie. 'Oh – except that he was wearing Wellington boots. They looked the same as Daddy's boots!'

'So it *was* one of them!' said Jack crossly.

'One of who?' asked Susie.

'Nothing to do with you!' snapped Jack. 'And don't you dare go telling anyone else what you've just seen, or it'll be the worse for you!'

'What's the big secret?' Binkie teased him. 'I say, you *do* like mysteries, don't you! Silly old Secret Seven!'

'Oh, very funny! Keep trying, and you may actually make a joke some day!' said Colin sarcastically. 'Come on, Jack,' he added, turning back to the shed. 'It won't be any use chasing the man now – he must be well away by this time.'

They joined the others in the shed, and saw that everyone was looking very solemn! In silence, Peter held out the letter that had been in the envelope the man had slipped under the door.

Jack and Colin looked at it, and saw that it was made up of letters cut out of a newspaper, and clumsily stuck together on a piece of paper. It said:

49

IF YOU KIDS GO INTARFEARING IN OUR BUSINES AGAIN YOUD BETER WHATCH OUT

'The cowards!' said George.

'So *that's* why they didn't burgle the grocer's shop after all!' said Jack. 'They know we know about them – and they're keeping us under observation.'

'They're not very good at spelling, are they?' said Peter, who was frowning over the letter.

'No, they're not!' Colin agreed. 'They're jolly good at running, though – even wearing Wellington boots!'

'Just think, all the time we were having our meeting, Susie and Binkie were wandering around quite close to our shed!' said Janet crossly.

'Never mind about that,' said Colin. 'For once, they've been quite useful. We'd never have known any more about the intruder if he hadn't passed them.'

Suddenly, there was a loud knock on the door of the shed! The children all held their breath. Had the writer of the anonymous letter come back? Was it Susie or Binkie trying to get in? Or their friend the police inspector? Though if they were to believe Mr Dunning, the inspector might not be feeling as friendly as usual today! All sorts of ideas came into their heads.

'Password?' asked Peter.

'Er – blackberry jelly!' said his mother, outside the

door. She laughed. Of course, that wasn't really the Seven's password, but they all knew her voice, and they sighed with relief. 'I came to ask if you'd pick me some blackberries tomorrow so that I can make jelly,' she added.

'Oh yes, we will!' said the Seven. Mother's blackberry jelly was simply delicious! And going blackberrying sounded rather more fun, just now, than deciphering mysterious messages.

Chapter Seven

PICKING BLACKBERRIES

After school next day, the Seven met at five o'clock just outside the village. They were carrying buckets and basins to hold the blackberries they were going to pick. With Scamper in the lead, they set off towards the old mill from which the farmhouse took its name. They knew there were some really good blackberry bushes up on the hill. They had decided to cut across the fields and then go up the little hillside paths used by the cows and sheep.

But though they all wanted to pick lots of ripe, juicy blackberries, they couldn't help thinking of that anonymous letter, and the mystery of who had written it and the note that Pam and Barbara had found in Mill Lane.

'I didn't sleep a wink all night,' said Pam. 'I felt sure there was somebody roaming around outside, underneath my window.' She shuddered dramatically.

'Come off it, Pam!' Colin grinned. 'If you go on like that, you'll find you're looking under your bed to see if there's anyone there next. And pretty soon you'll be wanting to sleep in your parents' bed with them, just as if you were a baby.'

Pam made a face at him, but Jack interrupted before they could start a real quarrel.

'Listen, one thing's certain – we *are* being watched! And the people keeping us under observation – whoever they are – have threatened to harm us. Golly, I wonder if they're watching us at this very moment?'

The children had just reached the bottom of the hill where the old mill stood. Its tall grey tower rose above the fields like a lighthouse. The way towards it was along a little path with high banks on either side. All of the children knew this place very well – yet suddenly the thought of being watched made them feel a little frightened.

'I'm scared!' Janet whispered.

'Me too,' Barbara admitted in a timid little voice.

'There's nothing to worry about!' said Peter firmly. 'We're in no danger so long as we don't interfere with these people, whoever they are – and as we haven't got a single clue about them at the moment, there's no way we *can* interfere.'

'Peter's right,' said George. 'Anyway, they can hardly be watching us night and day, can they? I don't suppose they're a bit interested in a black-berrying expedition.'

'But I know who *is* interested in a blackberrying expedition,' groaned Colin. 'Just look who's coming down the hill!'

Susie and Binkie had come round the corner of the path. The two little girls came to meet the Seven – holding baskets full of blackberries and smiling broadly!

'Those two little pests again!' said Pam. 'Can't we go *anywhere* without bumping into them?'

'I bet Susie heard me ask my parents if I could stay out late this evening picking blackberries,' said Jack. 'Ooh, she'll be sorry for this!'

By now, Susie and Binkie were close enough to hear what Jack was saying. 'Calm down, dear

brother!' Susie told him. 'There are lots of black-berries left. Plenty for everyone.'

'We only wanted to get here first so as to have the very best ones – and the ones that are easiest to pick,' said Binkie, aggravatingly. 'But you'll be able to find all you want so long as you don't mind getting your fingers pricked!'

Anyone would have thought Scamper understood the way the little girls were teasing his friends! He was leaping around them, showing his teeth and growling.

'I say, would one of you call that dog off?' said Susie in her shrill voice. 'We want to go on along the path!'

'All right, Scamper, that'll do!' said Peter.

The good dog immediately stopped jumping round Susie and Binkie and came back to his master. The two little girls stalked off without another word.

'The sheer cheek of it!' said George indignantly.

'I say, would one of you call that dog off?' Colin repeated, imitating Susie's voice – and at that Scamper took off like lightning after the two little pests! In panic, they started to run, and scurried away across the fields.

It was true that Susie and Binkie hadn't picked all the blackberries. The Seven found plenty on the bushes, and picked lots. They didn't even prick their fingers very badly, either!

Pam and Janet loved blackberries, and ate as many as they picked. The two greedy girls soon had mouths stained purple! As for the boys, they were having a race to see who could pick fastest. Peter had his bucket nearly full in less than half an hour.

The Seven were just thinking of starting back home when Colin gave an exclamation.

'Who do you think left *that* lying about? Honestly, I ask you! First the village, now here! It looks as if we ought to have litter-bins in the middle of the country-side too – ow!'

Colin had pricked himself. Peter and Jack turned to see their friend plunging into the middle of a bramble bush.

'What have you found, Colin?' asked Peter.

'An old newspaper – *ouch*! These brambles are simply full of thorns!' said Colin, wriggling into the very middle of the big bush.

'A newspaper?' said Peter, surprised. 'Fancy finding a newspaper out here.'

'Yes,' said Colin, from inside the bush. 'And it isn't an old one after all – it's hardly creased, and there hasn't been any rain or dew on it.'

'Then it can only just have been thrown away,' said Jack.

The brambles shook, and Colin came scrambling back to the path again, holding the newspaper in front of him – it was the first thing to appear from the middle of the trailing leaves! Colin himself came after

it, all hunched up as he tried to protect himself from the thorns.

'I say, that's rather odd, isn't it?' he said, straightening up. 'Why do you think anyone would throw away a brand-new newspaper, all neatly folded?'

'It *is* odd!' Peter agreed. 'People usually either keep their old newspapers in a pile, if they're going to want them for something, or they put them straight in the dustbin. I don't see why anybody would throw one away under a bramble bush in the middle of the country.'

Jack was looking at the newspaper. 'It's yesterday's local paper,' he said, unfolding it. 'Hallo – it's full of holes!' he added.

The boys looked at the newspaper in surprise. Sure enough, a lot of little square holes had been cut in it.

Hearing their excited exclamations, the three girls and George hurried up to join them. So did Scamper! He had got tired of chasing Susie and Binkie, and came panting along with his tongue hanging out.

Colin showed everyone his find.

'At nursery school, they taught us how to make cut-out paper doilies,' said Barbara, joking. 'This looks like a failed attempt at a doily!'

'I say – have you noticed?' said George. 'They only cut out big capital letters!'

'As if they wanted to use them to make new words,' said Janet.

'As if . . .' Jack began, but he never finished his

sentence, because Peter and Colin shouted, in chorus, 'The anonymous letter!'

Peter dug in his pocket for the note. He had kept it with him ever since it came under the door of the garden shed. Now he unfolded it again and spread it out on the grass.

'Colin, I'll read out the letters in the message,' he said. 'And you mark the places in the newspaper where you think they might have come. Here we go! I – F – Y – O . . .'

Peter read out the letters, and Colin underlined the holes in the newspaper at the places they might have come from. Leaning over the two of them, the others watched silently and intently. Their suspicions were being confirmed!

'. . . U – T!' Peter finished.

'. . . T!' said Colin. 'There – I've underlined spaces for all the cut-out letters, and everything would fit! They're the same as the letters used in the anonymous message!'

'So there's no doubt about it,' said Peter. 'This is the newspaper used by whoever wrote us that threatening note!'

'Oh, quick, let's hide it!' begged Pam in alarm.

'There's nothing to worry about,' George told her. 'They'd never expect us to find it. I'm sure they thought they'd hidden it safely.'

'If I was them I'd have burned it,' said Colin.

'So would I,' Peter agreed. 'Putting it here wasn't a

very clever thing to do!'

'It might have been,' said Barbara thoughtfully.

'What do you mean?' asked Jack.

'I mean this is just where I'd have hidden it if I *had* wanted it to be found!' Barbara explained.

'But *why* would they want us to find it?' asked Peter, puzzled.

'Well . . . I don't really know! All the same, doesn't it seem obvious? This newspaper pops up out of the ground at our feet, at the very moment when we can't go on investigating the mystery because we've run out of clues.'

'Yes,' said Janet, 'but you must admit it's an amazing coincidence, Barbara. I mean, suppose Mother had asked us to go and pick her some mushrooms instead . . . we wouldn't have been anywhere near this spot.'

'What you're getting at is that they must have *known* we were coming here to pick blackberries today!' said Pam. She was feeling more alarmed than ever. 'Oh, my goodness – they may be quite near us this very moment, spying on us!'

Chapter Eight

THE RUINED FARMHOUSE

Automatically, the Seven glanced round them. But all was quiet. They couldn't see anything but the trees and bushes, and the old mill on the hilltop.

'All the same, we must be careful,' said Peter. 'I think we'd better divide up. Jack and Colin, you come with me! We'll take Scamper and search by the side of the path. George, you and the girls go straight back to the main road and the village. If we're not back half an hour after you get home, you'd better tell our parents.'

Everyone agreed except Barbara.

'Can't I come searching with you, Peter?' she said. 'I mean, it was my idea that we were meant to find the newspaper!'

'Well, all right,' said Peter. 'You can come too – if you're sure you won't be frightened.'

Barbara wasn't a bit frightened now. She happily joined the boys.

George, Pam and Janet went straight down the hill to the main road, taking the buckets and basins of blackberries with them. Meanwhile, Peter, Jack, Colin and Barbara began searching. First of all they got Scamper to sniff the newspaper. The helpful spaniel was happy to oblige – but the result wasn't exactly what they expected. Scamper insisted on trying to go back to the village.

'He's not really interested in this newspaper,' said Peter. 'He wants to be with the others! Oh well – we'll just have to manage on our own!'

'Let's go a little way back up the path,' suggested Colin. 'We might find a trail there somewhere.'

Scamper was really being quite a nuisance – he *would* keep turning back towards the main road, and as he just wouldn't obey Peter, he had to go on his lead.

Going back uphill, the four children soon came to a place where two paths crossed and they couldn't go any farther, because the crossing was so muddy. There had been a lot of rain earlier that week, and the ground was all churned up by the hooves of the cows that passed over it.

'Just look at that mudbath!' said Jack. 'We'll never get through it! And there's no way of getting *round* it, either, with all those thorny bushes in the way.'

'You mean there's no way of getting round it or through it unless you have boots on,' said Colin, pointing. 'Look what *I've* seen! Footprints made by what look like the very same Wellingtons whose tracks we found in Mill Lane!'

'Oh yes – and there are the prints of the hill-walking boots too!' said Barbara.

'I say! This is our lucky day!' said Peter, pleased. 'Come on, let's take our shoes and socks off and wade through the mud in our bare feet. We can't let a little bit of mud stop us now!'

The others agreed. They could have kept their feet dry if they'd gone a long way round the muddy crossing, but they were short of time. It would be dark before very long, and the others would be expecting them back in the village. Anyway, wading through the mud barefoot would be fun, and more adventurous!

Soon there were four pairs of shoes and socks lined up beside the path. Splosh! Colin was the first to wade into the mud. It reached half-way up his calves. Jack and Barbara followed. They had to walk slowly and carefully, for fear of slipping. If they fell over, they'd be covered in mud from head to foot!

Finally Peter waded across, carrying Scamper. He wasn't going to leave his dog behind! They both reached the other side of the muddy crossing quite safely.

'We'll pick our shoes and socks up on the way back,' he said. 'Right – off we go, and mind where you tread!'

The four children did look funny with their muddy legs – as if they were wearing knee-length socks made of mud! Usually they'd have stopped to laugh at the

peculiar sight they presented, but just now they were in too much of a hurry to get on the trail of whoever was threatening them.

'And it should be quite easy!' said Colin. 'All we have to do is follow their footprints – they're clear enough!'

'How lucky they went through all that mud!' said Jack happily. 'That makes our job *much* easier!'

The footprints were certainly easy to spot. There were little dollops of mud left at regular intervals all along the grassy path, showing that the men wearing the boots had walked that way. Following the muddy prints, the four children found the trail was leading them to a lonely, deserted farmhouse. It had fallen partly into ruin, and was all overgrown with ivy. There were branches of trees growing in at the broken windows, and crows nesting among the chimney-pots.

'What a gloomy spot!' said Barbara. 'Brrr! I wouldn't like to be here on my own at night.'

'Well, you're not!' said Peter briskly. He always felt impatient with people who talked like that. 'You're here with us, and it's still light. Let's see if the place is really empty.'

He signalled to the others to get behind a bush near the house with him. They were careful not to make any noise. Then he picked up a few pebbles and threw them, aiming at the only door in the building which was still standing.

The pebbles whistled through the air and hit the door. Its wood was so rotten that the biggest pebbles splintered it, making a dull thudding sound.

The children crouched behind their bush, waiting to see if anything happened, but though they stayed there for several minutes, all was quiet.

'I'm going in!' Peter decided.

He went cautiously up to the old farmhouse and inside it, followed by Scamper. Jack, Colin and Barbara followed him. Soon they found themselves in a big, dark room. The only faint light filtered in through the ivy leaves that were growing over the one window.

Once the children's eyes were used to the dimness, they could make out a huge stone fireplace. Its hearth was all blackened. You could tell that cheerful, roaring fires must once have burned in that fireplace, and there were the remains of some nice tiles under a whole lot of rubbish.

Peter looked up and gave an exclamation.

'I say – owls!'

The others looked up too.

'Three of them!' said Jack.

Part of the ceiling had caved in, and the children could see a beam running across the hole, with three birds sitting very close together on it, as if it were a perch for them.

'They don't look very fierce, do they?' said Barbara.

'They're asleep,' Peter told her. 'We must leave them alone – they might attack us if they woke up, and anyway this is *their* home now! It's not fair to wake them up!'

'Look!' said Colin suddenly. 'We're not the first people to pay these owls a visit!'

He bent down and picked something up in one corner of the room. Then he showed his friends – there were several cigarette ends in the palm of his hand. Wessex Cigarettes!

'There must be at least fifty of them,' said Colin, looking at the rest of the cigarette ends in the corner. 'Those people spent quite a long time here!'

'I bet this is their headquarters!' said Jack. 'Did you notice the floor? It's got footprints all over it in the dust – as if they'd been pacing up and down here for hours on end!'

Scamper came over to sniff at the cigarette ends Colin had left on the floor. Then he began to growl, and showed his teeth.

'Oh, do let's hurry!' said Barbara. 'If the gang comes back we'll be trapped. That door's the only way out.'

Peter wasn't quite sure if she was right. He went over to the window and tried pushing back its thick curtain of ivy. But the branches wouldn't budge.

'Yes — we can't get out that way!' he admitted. 'The branches are as strong as bars on a prison window!'

'We could always hide upstairs,' said Colin. 'So long as part of the ceiling will still bear our weight, we wouldn't be so easily found up there.' He pointed. The ceiling had only caved in at one end of the room.

'Yes, the rest of the floor up there is probably all right,' Peter agreed. 'If it hasn't fallen in, that means the beams haven't rotted at that point. But we might as well go home now, so that we don't *have* to see if it'll hold us! I think we've seen all there is to see!'

'Goodnight, owls!' called Barbara, as they left the ruined house.

She was very glad to be out in the open again — whatever Peter said, she felt the old farmhouse had a very sinister atmosphere.

It was beginning to get darker now. Scamper and the four children went back along the path and reached the muddy crossing. They waded carefully over and retrieved their shoes and socks on the other side.

'Oh dear – we can't put them on, with our feet all covered in mud!' said Barbara. 'Golly, I'll be in hot water if I go home barefoot like this!'

Colin burst out laughing. 'Hot water is what we all *need* to be in! We could do with a bar of soap, too!'

'If we go the long way round, we'll pass the brook. We could wash our feet there,' Peter suggested.

'Let's do that,' Jack agreed. 'Come on – we must hurry if we want to be home before dark!'

So they set off at once, carrying their shoes and socks. Scamper ran happily along beside them. His lovely golden coat had hardly got muddy at all.

The brook wasn't too far away. The children had a quick wash in it, and Scamper drank some lovely cool spring water.

George, Pam and Janet were very relieved to see their friends arrive back in the village. They had been getting really worried, and were just about to raise the alarm.

Peter told them about the ruined farmhouse, and they decided that they would all go and lie in wait there next day, which was Saturday. Before they said good night and went to their own homes, they swore that they wouldn't mention what they had discovered to anyone. It was a funny thing, and rather worrying, but ever since that threatening letter had been slipped under the door of the garden shed, they just hadn't been able to shake off the feeling that they were being watched nearly all the time . . .

Chapter Nine

THOSE TWO LITTLE PESTS!

At two o'clock next day, the Seven were on the warpath!

They had decided not to take Scamper with them, in case he gave them away while they were in hiding. And they didn't want to wade through all that mud where the paths crossed again, so they went to the old farmhouse a different way. They cycled to the old mill, left their bicycles in a dry ditch there, and then cut through the woods on foot.

That meant they would be coming up to the back of the ruined house – so they weren't as likely to be spotted by anyone inside, who would expect people to come up the path to the front door, just as the four children had done the day before.

The thick carpet of moss in the woods meant they could go along in silence. Soon they saw the tumbledown chimneys of the old farm above the treetops. There were several crows flying round the chimney-pots, disturbing the silence with their noisy cawing.

'We'll get into a good position and then keep

watch,' said Peter softly. 'We must skirt round the building until we can see the doorway.'

'We may be in for a long wait,' said Colin. 'Suppose the people we're after never turn up at all?'

'They may not,' Peter admitted. 'But it *does* look as if this is their headquarters, so it's well worth waiting to see!'

'Why don't we go in and see if they've been back here since we visited the place yesterday?' asked Jack.

'Too dangerous,' Peter told him. 'They may be inside the house at this very moment.'

'Or they might turn up while *we* were inside it,' George said.

'Ooh – do you think they'll have guns with them?' asked Janet, feeling rather frightened.

'That's quite possible,' Colin said. Poor Janet didn't feel any better! The thought of that threatening letter was weighing on her mind. And even if they didn't like to admit it, the rest of the Seven were a little scared too!

Stealthily, they followed Peter as he went up to the ruined building and cautiously skirted round it. At last they came in sight of the door.

'Now, let's divide up,' Peter whispered. 'Colin and George, you go a little way down the path and hide beside it. You can act as scouts. If you see or hear anyone coming, throw a stone at the farmhouse wall – that's the signal to let us know!'

'All right,' said George.

'And whatever you do, don't move until I give the word!' Peter told the two boys. They went off down the path, and he turned to the girls. 'You three girls spread out between the path and the farmhouse. Then we can pass messages along a chain if we have to get in touch. Jack and I will stay here, closest to the house.'

'Fine,' said Barbara, and the three girls tiptoed away to get into position. Pam looked back and held up her crossed fingers to the boys, to wish them all luck.

That left Peter and Jack on their own by the house. They got underneath a big, spreading bush, and lay flat on the ground. They had a clear view of the farmhouse doorway.

The first hour seemed to pass quite quickly. The children waited in their positions and watched the crows circling the farmhouse chimneys. But after a while their wait began to get boring. Colin, who had wriggled his way into the middle of a hazel thicket, got out his penknife, cut himself a nice stout hazel stick, and began whittling away at it. George was lying flat on a big rock overlooking the path, so he had a view of the main road in the distance, and he amused himself by counting the cars that drove past.

As for the girls, Barbara started plaiting dry glasses together, and Pam and Janet played a game of throwing sweets at each other and catching them.

Sometimes they ate a sweet too!

Peter and Jack, however, kept on the alert the whole time. But nearly two hours passed by, and still there was no sign of life in or near the farmhouse! They were almost sure by now that there was nobody inside it. Would anyone turn up?

Another hour passed, and *still* nothing happened.

Colin's legs were beginning to feel stiff and cramped, because he couldn't stretch them. George felt as if he were getting hypnotized by the sight of the cars driving past in the distance. And the girls had started chattering to each other. Barbara was holding up the little grass basket she had woven to show the others.

'Ssh!' Peter hissed at them angrily, from his own hiding-place.

And all was quiet again.

Another fifteen minutes went by – and then, suddenly, a small stone struck the farmhouse wall. Peter and Jack jumped.

'It's the signal!' Peter whispered.

Jack passed the message on to Janet, who was nearest to him. 'The signal!'

'The signal!' she told Pam in a soft voice.

And so the message went back along the chain until it reached George, who had thrown the stone in the first place.

He had heard voices, and knew someone must be coming along the path, so he clambered down from the big rock to find a stone to throw and warn his friends. Now he couldn't see the path itself any more – but Colin, who was in position further along the pathway, was keeping his eyes wide open. And the three girls, stationed closer to the farmhouse, were feeling very excited. Flat on the ground under their bush, Jack and Peter held their breath. They had their ears pressed close to the ground, so they could hear the approaching footsteps quite clearly. Soon they too heard voices. What sort of people would appear round the corner of the path? The children were all longing to know! In a moment or so that part of the mystery, at least, would be solved!

By now the sun was sinking low, and the shadows were getting longer. Two tall shadows were the first things that Peter and Jack saw, as they were cast on the farmhouse wall. The two boys narrowed their eyes, and turned to look down the pathway and into the setting sun. The mysterious strangers were walking slowly – their footsteps sounded heavy. Any moment now they would come into sight . . .

'Oh no! *Susie*!' said Jack, between his teeth.

'Shut up!' Peter hissed.

Those two little pests Susie and Binkie were walking along the pathway up to the farmhouse, dragging their feet – because they were wearing men's boots!

Susie was wearing Wellington boots. One glance told Jack that they were Fisherman brand

74

Wellington boots – his father's own pair! And Binkie was wearing a pair of hill-walking boots which Peter guessed belonged to her big brother.

So *they* were behind the mystery! The two little girls had written that note Pam and Barbara had found in Mill Lane – just to make the Secret Seven think someone was planning to burgle the grocer's shop! And they had written the anonymous letter too. That accounted for the bad spelling. They had put the newspaper with the missing letters where they knew the Seven would find it, and laid a false trail of cigarette ends to make them think there was a gang of criminals about. The men's footprints were all part of their plan too.

Jack was simply boiling with rage. He thought back over all the things that had happened over the last few days. *Now* he knew why those two pests happened to be so close when the Seven tried to catch whoever had slipped the anonymous letter under the door of the garden shed! Now he knew why they were on their way home from picking blackberries just as the Seven reached the blackberry bushes! Now he knew why Scamper kept barking and wanted to follow the two little girls back to the village! It all made sense.

What a horrible hoax! Susie and Binkie had made the Seven look silly – but they'd be sorry for it! Jack imagined himself coming up behind Susie and cutting off her pigtails . . . and shaving Binkie bald as

an egg! He could think of worse things he'd like to do to them, too. He thought what fun it would be to hang them up in the trees in cages without any food or water, until they begged for mercy! Oh dear – he just couldn't stand it any longer! Jack felt he must do *something* or burst.

He half rose to his feet, to rush out and confront the two little girls, but Peter firmly pushed him down again.

'Keep still!' he ordered in a whisper. 'We'll have the last laugh, don't you worry!'

Jack closed his eyes, took a deep breath, and tried to relax. It wasn't easy, when he had those two grinning little faces so close. Well, he'd bide his time – his revenge would be all the sweeter in the end!

At last Susie and Binkie reached the farmhouse. They were carrying big shopping bags.

'Golly!' sighed Susie, pushing the farmhouse door open. 'It's tiring work walking about in these boots.'

The two girls went inside, but they left the door wide open, so Peter and Jack could still hear what they were saying.

'How much longer are we going on with this game?' asked Binkie, whining a little. 'I'm getting blisters on my feet!'

'I suppose it may go on for quite a long time yet!' said Susie. 'Those silly things are simply hopeless at investigating mysteries. They think they're such wonderful detectives – and goodness knows we've given them lots and lots of clues!'

'No, they aren't very clever,' Binkie agreed. 'Oh, won't they look silly! I can just imagine Peter's face. He's so conceited – he'll hate to think he's been tricked so easily!' And she laughed like anything.

Lying under the bush, Peter was seething with

fury.

'Oh, look – they must have found the cigarette ends, anyway,' said Susie. 'At least, some of them are missing. Luckily they haven't taken them *all*. At this rate my father isn't going to be able to provide me with enough!'

'Has he seen you emptying the ashtrays?' asked Binkie.

'Yes, he has – but I told him I was tidying up to help Mummy, and he said I was a good little girl!' And that horrible Susie burst out laughing.

Lying in hiding, Jack had to clench his fists hard to keep himself from shouting at her.

Inside the house, the two little girls were still talking.

'We'll let them go on stewing in their own juice today,' Susie decided. 'And then, tomorrow, we'll send them another message – something really blood-curdling!'

'I'm a bit scared in case they turn up *now*,' Binkie admitted. 'That tall boy looks awfully fierce sometimes!'

'You mean Colin?' said Susie. 'Oh, don't worry, he's feeble, just like the rest of them! There's nothing to worry about. Jack told me they were all going to help Peter and Janet's mother make blackberry jelly this afternoon.'

Jack couldn't help smiling. It had been a stroke of genius to think of telling his sister that story.

Through the branches of the bush, he saw the two little pests come out of the farmhouse again. Peter leaned over and whispered in Jack's ear, 'Now whatever you do, don't move! Our turn will come!'

The little girls started off along the path, but Binkie soon stopped.

'I'm sick and tired of dragging myself about in these clodhoppers,' she whined. 'Can't we take them off for the walk home?'

'Oh, all right,' said Susie. 'But mind you walk on the grass beside the path. We don't want them to see our real footprints!'

So the two little pests took off the big men's boots they were wearing and put them in their shopping bags. They had their own shoes on inside the boots. Then they went off, still laughing.

Now Jack and Peter understood why their baskets had looked so full of blackberries the day before. The boots were underneath, and there was just a layer of blackberries on top to hide them!

The two boys waited a moment before emerging from their bush. Once they were sure Susie and Binkie were out of hearing distance, they joined the others.

'Honestly, those horrible girls! How *could* they?' asked Janet indignantly.

Pam and Barbara were so furious they couldn't speak at all. George was white in the face with rage. Colin was thinking grimly that he had a bone to pick with Susie. Fancy having the cheek to call him feeble!

'Now, calm down, everyone!' Peter said, as his friends spluttered with anger. 'Don't get carried away! We'll have our revenge – and I can tell you it will be a jolly good revenge too. But we need clear heads to plan it properly.'

All the way home, the Secret Seven were discussing what to do. And by the time they reached the village, they had settled what their plan was to be! It was something that those two awful little pests certainly wouldn't forget in a hurry . . .

Chapter Ten

THE SEVEN PLAN REVENGE

Some rather odd things happened that Saturday
evening.

At nine o'clock a passer-by might have seen Peter,
George and Colin walking down the High Street. Or
rather, a passer-by might *not* have seen them, because
they were avoiding any brightly-lit spots, and if they
heard anyone coming, they darted into a dark doorway or alley. They were wearing dark-coloured
clothes, and soft-soled shoes. They didn't want to be
noticed.

At last they arrived at their school. The buildings
were empty at this time of night. There wasn't any
sound to be heard beyond the playground wall, and
there was no light in any of the windows except a faint
bluish glimmer coming from the caretaker's flat.

'He's watching television,' said Peter, in relief. 'So
that's all right – he won't hear anything!'

'He might if he's watching an old silent film!'
whispered Colin, with a laugh.

George frowned at him. This was no time for joking!

The three boys waited, crouching down between two parked cars, to make sure the coast was clear. They heard the sound of gunshots from the care-taker's flat, and Peter winked at the others. The Saturday night film on television must be a Western or a gangster picture. 'We're in luck!' he whispered. 'We could break the door down and not be heard!'

He gave one last glance round, and signalled to George and Colin to go ahead.

They all hurried over to the foot of the wall en-closing the playground. Colin leaned back against it and joined his hands to make a step for Peter to stand on. Peter used it to help hoist himself up on Colin's shoulders and then on top of the wall. He steadied himself, and then jumped down into the playground.

George followed – but before jumping down on the other side of the wall, he stopped to haul Colin up after him, and then they both jumped down together.

Peter didn't want to hang around. He led them straight off to the left-hand wing of the school building. They walked on the grass rather than the gravel paths, so that they wouldn't make any noise. The science laboratories were in the left-hand wing. The boys passed the physics and chemistry labs, and soon got to the biology lab.

This was where they were going!

'Now, let's hope there's a window open!' whispered Peter.

They crept cautiously over to the lab. To their relief, there *was* a window open. Colin had remembered that on Friday afternoon, the biology master had opened it at the end of a lesson, to let out the nasty smells coming from some chemicals stored in a little room next door. And no one had closed it again.

So it was quite easy for them to climb in! They knew their way round the lab, so they didn't have to risk putting a light on. And anyway, there was moonlight coming in through a skylight in the lab roof. It cast a weird glow over a row of jars lined up on a shelf. George gasped as he suddenly found himself face to face with a snake pickled in formaldehyde! He was quite used to seeing it in the daytime – but it looked almost alive at night, in the moonlight.

The three boys went over to the back of the laboratory. They found what they were looking for. And when they left the lab again, they were carrying something quite large, wrapped in a big black cloth . . .

Whatever *could* it be?

Janet and Pam were dressmaking that evening, up in Janet's attic bedroom, with its sloping roof. Only it was a rather odd sort of dressmaking! Janet had asked her mother for some old sheets that had worn out and been turned sides to middle, and then had worn thin again so that they weren't any use as bedclothes any more. The two girls were busy cutting them up.

'My word – it's harder than you might think, cutting a really round hole!' said Janet.

'Careful!' Pam advised her. 'Mind you don't make it too big!'

Janet tried really hard, putting the tip of her tongue between her teeth as she concentrated on her work, and at last she managed to cut two round holes, each about the size of a five pence piece.

'Now what?' she asked her friend.

'Now you make the bottom all raggedy, like this!'

Pam showed what she meant. She made a cut with her scissors at the edge of the sheet and then tore it a little way. 'And several more like that!' she said. 'It will look really effective!'

Scamper barked, as if he wanted to show that he agreed, and Janet started cutting and tearing her own sheet.

Meanwhile Barbara was in her parents' garage, where her father kept his tools. She was getting exhausted! She had opened all sorts of cases and boxes to see what was inside them. Her hands were covered with oil, and she was hot and dusty. But still she hadn't found what she was looking for.

She was feeling rather discouraged by the time she opened the fifth big tool-box. But then her face lit up with a big grin. Here they were at last!

She brought out four long chains, and put them on her father's work-bench. Now she only had to paint them . . .

Jack was the only one of the Seven who *looked* as if he was acting normally that evening. He was sitting with his parents and his sister watching television. However, it would be a mistake to think he was doing nothing while his friends were all hard at work. It might not show, but he had one of the most important jobs of all. He was keeping watch on Susie!

When the programme they had been watching was

over, he said good night to his mother and father and went up to his bedroom. Susie followed him. On the stairs, that little pest had the nerve to ask him how the Seven were getting on with the mystery they were trying to solve.

'When will you be getting the police to arrest the criminals?' she asked pertly.

'Not just yet, I'm afraid!' said Jack. He tried to look puzzled. 'We can't seem to find enough clues.'

'Fancy that!' said Susie. She didn't even bother to hide her grin. Jack could hear her giggling as she went into her own room.

He locked himself in *his* bedroom and flung himself on his bed, thumping his pillow with his fists to let off steam. Honestly, he didn't think he could bear it! He had had a perfectly horrible evening, pretending not to know anything, while all the time his hands were itching to get at that horrible little sister of his. Well, by this time tomorrow he'd have settled accounts with *her*!

He got up to draw his curtains before he went to bed. But as he was drawing them, he thought he saw a light flashing in the garden. Jack was just telling himself that he must have been imagining things, when the light flashed again, lighting up the whole garden for a second. He waited a moment or so, and realised that the flash was coming at regular intervals. Cautiously he put out the electric light in his own room and leaned out of the window. How surprised he was to see Susie, at *her* window, flashing Morse code with her torch!

Jack kept quite still. The moon had gone behind clouds, and it was very dark now, so Susie couldn't see him. Luckily he knew Morse code, and could decipher the message his sister was flashing.

In long and short flashes of light, she was saying, 'Meet me at the Sunday market tomorrow. Then we'll discuss Operation Silly Seven. Good night. Susie.'

Jack was so furious about that 'Operation Silly Seven' he nearly didn't notice a bright point of light winking on and off in reply from a house in the road opposite.

'Fine. We meet at the basket stall at nine o'clock. Good night. Binkie.'

Then he heard Susie close her window. That dear little girl was in for a big surprise tomorrow!

Chapter Eleven

BACK TO THE FARMHOUSE

The market Susie meant was a big Sunday market which was held in the village most weekends. It was a cheerful, noisy occasion. People from the nearby farms brought their produce to sell, and there were several craft stalls too. One of these belonged to a basket-maker.

Jack reached the market early, at ten to nine. He stood watching the basket-maker at work. There were dozens and dozens of finished baskets piled up on the stall, and the man's nimble fingers were busy with yet another. He was so clever at it that several people stopped to watch. Among them, Jack noticed the young man who had been to his house collecting for charity – the same collector as he had seen again outside school on Thursday morning. He still had a box, which he was shaking hopefully under the noses of passers-by. Jack couldn't help thinking that by now almost everybody in the village must have given a contribution. But perhaps the man was hoping to collect more money from people who came to the market from farther away.

At two minutes to nine Binkie arrived. When she saw Jack she looked away and pretended not to have seen him.

At one minute to nine, Susie joined her. The two little girls linked arms and went off into the crowd. Jack started following them. Susie turned round and gave him a nasty look. Then she suddenly did an about-turn, and led Binkie up an alleyway between rows of stalls. By the time Jack had turned too and started after them, the two girls had disappeared. However, he soon found them again. They were sitting on the ground, hiding behind a tall pyramid of plastic hampers containing lettuces!

'Oh, really! Why don't you leave us alone?' complained Susie, in her shrill voice.

'If we needed a bodyguard we'd choose a stronger one than you!' added Binkie.

Jack only grinned. 'Little girls oughtn't to go for walks on their own!' he told them. 'It might be dangerous! So I'm going to keep my dear little sister company wherever she goes today — it will be my good deed!'

'What — *all* day today?' said Binkie.

'Well, till six o'clock, anyway,' said Jack. 'The Secret Seven Society are all going to the cinema this evening.'

'All right, Binkie — we'll meet again at six,' Susie

told her friend. 'You'd better go home now. I don't suppose *you* want to trail round with Jack all day!'

And the two little pests said goodbye, winking hard at each other! Perhaps they thought Jack wouldn't notice!

Susie didn't say a single word to her brother as they walked home from the Sunday market. But as they passed the church they saw a charity collector standing outside, waiting for people to come out of the service, and Susie muttered, 'That man again – he's always begging!'

Jack looked more closely, and saw that it was the young man he'd seen at Peter and Janet's house. So *he* was still here with his collecting-box too. It looked as if their village must be famous for its generosity!

As he walked off with Susie, he could hear the man jingling the money in his box.

Susie didn't enjoy that Sunday one little bit. Her brother stuck close to her and wouldn't leave her alone for a second. Even when she said she was going to her own room, he said he'd keep her company. Susie was furious, but her parents thought Jack was being very nice to her for once, so she couldn't be as nasty to him as she wanted.

The afternoon seemed endless. It was very boring for Jack too – Susie could tell, and at least *that* amused her!

When the clock struck six, both of them were

90

relieved.

Jack picked up his jacket and ran straight out of the house, saying that he must go or he'd be late for the cinema.

Susie wasn't in so much of a hurry. While she waited for Binkie, she sat down at her desk, unlocked a drawer, and took out a little notebook. She tore a page out of it, and wrote, in capital letters:

FINEL WORNING! IF YOU SET FOOT HEER ONCE MORE YOUR LIVES WIL NOT BE WURTH A PENNY!

Susie put her pen down and read what she had written. She felt very pleased with it!

Jack met his friends just outside the village. Of course they weren't really going to the cinema — Jack had just *said* so, to put Susie off the scent! The Seven set off for the old farmhouse. They hoped and expected to see Susie and Binkie there too, before very long. And then there would be a very interesting little entertainment!

The daylight was beginning to fade. Peter led the party. George and Colin came behind him, carrying the object wrapped in black cloth that they had 'borrowed' from school. Pam and Janet followed, with bundles of white sheets. Jack and Barbara brought up the rear. They were carrying a heavy canvas bag between them, each holding one handle.

They had so much to carry that they couldn't ride their bicycles, and had to go on foot – but they still went up to the old mill and then cut through the woods, to avoid the muddy crossing.

The sun was low on the horizon when they reached the ruined farmhouse. Peter switched on his torch, to show them all the way in. He walked into the ruins first, and the others followed, except for George and Colin. They stayed outside, with whatever it was they had wrapped in that black cloth.

There was a surprise waiting for the children when

they got inside the big room.

'Look – someone's been having a fire!' said Janet, pointing to a heap of ash and cinders in the hearth.

'And there are some empty cans in this corner of the room!' said Barbara. 'I'm sure *they* weren't here yesterday!'

'I expect Binkie put them there,' said Peter. 'We know Susie didn't get a chance to shake Jack off all day – but Binkie could have come here this afternoon to plant some more of their precious "clues" for us.'

'Oh, what a pity – that means they may not come at all this evening,' said Pam. 'And we had *such* a fine reception planned for them!'

'Oh, they'll come!' said Jack. 'She's as stubborn as a donkey. I could tell she wanted to come here – and once she's made up her mind to do something, there's no stopping her!'

'Well, let's hurry up and get ready!' said Peter.

Janet and Pam gave out the cut-up sheets they had brought with them. 'And these two are for George and Colin, outside,' said Pam, handing Peter two extra sheets.

'Here are the chains,' said Barbara. She took the four chains out of the canvas bag. They were all silvery now. 'Be careful – the paint's not quite dry in some places.'

When the sheets and chains had been given out, Jack and the three girls went upstairs. They took great care not to go near the part where the floor had caved in over the room below.

'Quick – you must get into costume!' said Peter. He shone his torch up the stairs to give them a bit of light. There was a lot of flapping as the sheets were unfolded – and a moment or so later, instead of Jack, Pam, Barbara and Janet, Peter saw four ghosts in white robes, carrying silver chains that flashed light.

'That's fine!' said Peter. 'You look terrific! See you soon, then – and mind you're really frightening!'

He went out of the house again. The four ghosts were invisible upstairs in the dark now that Peter's torch was turned off them.

Outside the farmhouse, Peter, George and Colin went off to the shelter of some thick bushes, put the black cloth and whatever was inside it down on the grass, and lost no time in getting into their own ghost costumes. Then, with a dramatic sweep of his arm, Peter flung back the black wrappings to reveal – a skeleton!

'Hallo, Archie!' he said. 'I hope you're not too tired after the journey?'

Colin grinned, and patted the skeleton on its shoulder-blade in a friendly way. 'He *does* look tired – worn to the bone!'

'And a bit hollow-cheeked!' said George, laughing.

'Well, he'll be all right, and we shall return him to the biology lab safe and sound!' said Peter.

Just then they heard voices – Susie and Binkie were coming along the path!

'Ssh!' whispered Peter. 'The fun's about to begin!'
The three boys lay flat on the ground beside
Archie, the school skeleton. The first thing they saw
was the light of two torches. Then Susie and Binkie
walked past, quite close to them. They had men's
heavy boots on again. They went into the ruined
house without suspecting anything!

Jack and the three girls had an excellent view from the upstairs room. They had to pinch their noses under their sheet costumes to stop themselves bursting into laughter. The idea was that they would wait for a few moments, before appearing to 'haunt' the two little pests. That would make it even more of a surprise!

But nobody knew what the *really* big surprise was going to be . . .

'Hallo — where did those cans come from?' said Binkie in surprise, seeing the empty tin cans in one corner.

'Oh, look — somebody's lit a fire in the hearth!' said Susie.

'Who can it have been?' asked Binkie, sounding worried.

'Just that silly Secret Seven Society,' Susie guessed. 'It *is* odd, though! I mean, I know Jack was at home all day.'

'Oh dear — I don't quite like this,' said Binkie, sounding even more worried. 'Don't let's wait — let's go straight home again!'

In the upstairs room, the four 'ghosts' were beginning to wonder if something else was up, too.

The two little girls hastily set to work to leave their 'clues' for the Seven to find. Susie gave Binkie a box full of cigarette ends to scatter round the room. Then she took the note she had written out of her pocket, and stuck it on the fireplace with chewing-gum.

Then Susie and Binkie turned to leave the ruined house – and as they did so, they heard the sound of a motor-bike, quite close, coming along the path to the farmhouse.

Chapter Twelve

EVERYONE GETS A SURPRISE

The two little girls stood rooted to the ground.

'There's somebody coming!' wailed Binkie.

'Quick – let's hide over in this corner!' said Susie.

The two girls put out their torches and ran into the darkest corner of the room. As for the 'ghosts' in the room above, *they* were puzzled and scared as well!

There was a backfiring, spluttering noise as the motor-bike came up the path. Suddenly the bright light of its headlamp lit up the outside of the farmhouse. The bike swept past quite close to Peter, George and Colin. The three boys lay as flat as they could, to keep out of the beam of its headlamp. They could make out the shapes of two men on the bike. It stopped at the farmhouse door, and the engine was switched off. The two men dismounted and went straight into the ruin.

'They were carrying something,' whispered Peter.

'I don't think it looked like guns,' said Colin.

'No – more like boxes of some sort,' agreed George.

Indoors, the two motor-cyclists switched on

torches. The four ghosts, and the two little girls in the corner, nearly cried out in surprise. The newcomers were the two young men who had been so busy collecting for the blind and for deprived children!

As soon as they had shut the door behind them, they burst into laughter. They thought something was very funny indeed! As they gasped for air, they rattled their collecting-boxes, and that set them off laughing again. From the sound of the collecting-boxes, they must have been full to the brim.

'We diddled everyone nicely!' gasped one of the young men at last.

'Yes – fancy believing us so easily, when we said we were collecting for charity!'

'We've got those forged cards saying we're authorised to collect, of course, but almost nobody asked to see them!'

The four 'ghosts' on the floor above drew together. Barbara, Pam and Janet were trembling underneath their sheets. Jack was worried about his little sister, down there with those two unpleasant young men. They might find Susie and Binkie any moment! What would happen next? The Seven had planned to play a trick on the two little pests to get their own back – but they didn't want them to run into any *real* danger! This was terrible.

Susie and Binkie, crouching in their corner, were terrified. They weren't boasting of their own clever-ness any more, as they listened to the two unscrupulous collectors talking about *theirs*!

'How gullible some people can be!'

'Well, now we've got all we can out of *that* village, I suggest we go collecting for the blind somewhere else!'

And the two young men laughed again.

But suddenly they stopped short. They had just caught sight of Susie's message, stuck to the fireplace. One of them read it out.

' "Final warning! If you set foot here once more, your lives will not be worth a penny!" '

'What on earth does that mean?' asked the other, sounding alarmed.

'I told you so!' said his friend, angrily. 'I said this wasn't a good spot for our base! We never ought to have come back here this evening!'

'Look – more cigarette ends on the floor! Like the ones we saw yesterday!' said the other man, shining his torch on the floor.

'Let's get out of here!' said his friend.

'No – wait a minute!' said the man with the torch. 'I think *I* can solve the mystery!' And he swept the torch round until its light fell on the two little girls in the corner.

'Well, well, well! Give us a final warning, would you?' he said, roaring with laughter. And then he suddenly shouted, 'Get out of here – get out at once, or you'll be sorry!'

Binkie and Susie were so scared they couldn't even

move! The man came closer to them, saying angrily, 'Go on, or I'll skin you alive!'

'No – wait!' said his friend. 'We can't let them get away – they'll go straight down to the village and set the police on our trail!'

Suddenly Susie and Binkie managed to move – they dashed for the door, but the young man who had just spoken stopped them. 'Oh no, you don't!' he said. Susie wriggled out of his grasp – but by now his friend was between her and the door! She and Binkie were trapped. The door was the only possible way out of the room.

Upstairs, the four 'ghosts' had made their way cautiously to the edge of the hole where the ceiling had caved in, and were looking down. There was nothing they could do to help Susie and Binkie – they felt powerless! Peter and George and Colin, out in the bushes, had heard what was going on inside, and they felt just the same. It was infuriating not to be able to do anything to help!

'There's no time to go down to the village for help! Oh, blow!' whispered Colin.

'We'll never manage to rescue them – just the three of us!' said George. 'Those two men are much bigger than we are!'

'We'll manage all right!' said Peter suddenly. 'I've had an idea!'

Inside the house, the two men had found some old bits of rope lying round the room, and were busy tying Susie and Binkie up.

'There – you won't get away so easily now!' said one of them sarcastically, pulling the knot round Binkie's hands tighter.

'And by the time you raise the alarm we'll be well away!' said the other. He had poor Susie trussed up like a chicken!

The two little girls didn't say a word – it was bad enough being tied up like this, but they'd been afraid even worse might happen to them.

However, as the two men were turning to leave the house, Binkie gave a shrill scream.

'Help! A ghost!' she cried, terrified.

'What? What's your game, little girl?' asked one of the young men suspiciously.

'I saw a ghost – up there, under the roof! Looking down through that hole in the ceiling!' said Binkie.

Her teeth were chattering.

'What nonsense! You don't take *us* in!' said the second young man angrily.

'Oh, there *is* a ghost!' wailed Susie, in her turn. 'Up there – I *saw* it! You can't leave us here – let us out! It'll kill us!' She was in a panic.

'Both of you seeing ghosts!' said the first young man. 'This is ridiculous!'

But he was interrupted by another piercing shriek from Binkie. The poor little girl was really frightened. She was twisting and turning in the ropes that held her. 'It's up there! I can see it – it's looking at me!'

The two young men both looked up – and to their amazement, they saw the ghost too! It was in the room above, looking down on them from the edge of the hole in the ceiling, waving a white winding sheet about in the air!

Jack was really throwing himself whole-heartedly into his performance. He let his silvery chains whistle through the air within a whisker of the men's noses.

'Help – there's something very strange about this place!' said one of the young men in a rather shaky voice. 'Let's get out!'

And then there was a knock on the door – or rather, three knocks, very loud and clear.

The two men stood perfectly still, looking at each other in alarm. Susie and Binkie were doing their best not to cry out – but they couldn't help it when they saw one of the men suddenly produce a knife. It looked very sharp.

'I'll open the door,' he told his friend in a low voice. 'And if there's any trouble, you can come and help me.'

Cautiously, making no noise and taking all sorts of precautions, he went to the door, took hold of the latch, and flung it open all of a sudden.

Archie, who was waiting outside, toppled in!

Terrified, the young man instinctively flung the skeleton away from him, and it fell towards his companion, who was coming to help him. Archie's long, bony arms were thrown round the second young man's neck! They made a clattering noise like castanets.

Up in their hiding-place, Pam, Janet, Barbara and Jack were watching in surprise and delight. Who'd have thought, only a few moments ago, that the tables could be turned so well?

The second young man was howling with terror now, as he tried to free himself from the friendly skeleton! When at last he managed to do so, he didn't wait for any more. He dashed out of the house. His friend was outside already.

'Oh no! The tyres are flat!' he shouted angrily as the second young man joined him. 'This place is bewitched!' We'd better run for it, before it's too late.'

But as they took to their heels, the two men saw three ghosts emerge from the bushes! Peter, George

and Colin came towards them, clanking their silver chains.

The two young men stopped short, stupefied, as they saw the ghosts advancing. Then they turned and ran off into the night – it looked as if they'd be beating the Olympic sprinting record!

Now the house was empty, and all the three boys had to do was walk in.

They found that the torches dropped by the two men were lighting up the room, casting enormous shadows on the walls. The place looked like something out of a horror film. Susie and Binkie were lying quite still on the floor, too frightened even to scream as they saw the new ghosts come in. But their eyes were popping out of their heads! The three boys did a little dance about them, pretending to wail in a very ghostly way – though they could hardly stop giggling! The other four children came downstairs to join in the dance. Susie and Binkie just stared. They couldn't make it out – though they were beginning to feel there was something familiar about the ghosts. And when they wailed and chanted, their voices sounded a bit *too* lifelike. The owls had been woken by all the noise, and came fluttering down to see what was going on – but even the owls seemed puzzled!

'All right, everyone – that'll do!' said Peter, taking off his sheet. And the rest of the Secret Seven took off their own costumes too.

It was just too much for poor little Susie and Binkie, and they burst into tears!

Well, those two little pests had had their punishment, and they promised never to play such a nasty trick on the Secret Seven again!

As for the young men who had been pretending to collect for charity, they were arrested a few days later. The Seven had given the police a lot of useful, detailed information about them. The inspector told the children that the money collected for charity on false pretences really *would* go to the blind and to deprived children now.

'But the parish council would like to give you a reward,' said the friendly inspector. 'They're grateful to you for catching people who cheated so many of the villagers. What do you suggest the reward should be?'

The children had a quick consultation, and then Peter turned to the inspector again.

'Would the parish council give the village a couple of litter-bins?' he asked.

'They could be painted green, so they wouldn't look out of place,' added Jack.

'I think that sounds like a very good idea!' said the inspector. 'And I'm sure the parish council will be happy to agree!'

And so they were! From now on, there would be no excuse at all for anyone to leave mysterious messages

lying about in the village where the Secret Seven
lived . . .

If you have enjoyed this book, you may like to
read some more exciting adventures
from Knight Books:

A complete list of new adventures
about the SECRET SEVEN

KNIGHT BOOKS

A complete list of the SECRET SEVEN ADVENTURES by Enid Blyton

KNIGHT BOOKS

A complete list of the FAMOUS FIVE ADVENTURES by Enid Blyton

KNIGHT BOOKS